DUEL MASTERS™

KAIJUDO MASTER'S GUIDE

Michael Searle

SCHOLASTIC INC.

New York   Toronto   London   Auckland   Sydney

Mexico City   New Delhi   Hong Kong   Buenos Aires

ISBN 0-439-69113-3

Published by Scholastic Inc.
SCHOLASTIC and associated logos are trademarks and/or registered trademarks of Scholastic Inc.

12 11 10 9 8 7 6 5 4 3 2 1   5 6 7 8 9/0

Printed in the U.S.A.
First printing, March 2005

master the world

You can hold the trophy.

No matter how many Duel Masters cards you own or don't own.

No matter how old the other kids are at your local tournament.

No matter if you picked up your first booster pack yesterday and haven't yet memorized the difference between summoning sickness and shield triggers.

No matter what, this strategy guide will help you hold the shiny trophy that only champions get to raise in the winner's circle.

Once you've read up on Duel Masters' basic rules, our *Kaijudo Master's Guide* gives you a wealth of advanced strategy. See superior playing tips for the latest cards, take a crash course on deck-building for each civilization, train in the ways of tournament play, and enjoy the ride with a ton of super-cool puzzles.

Do us one favor, though: Send an autographed Mighty Shouter when you become world champion.

expert strategy

Olympic athletes train for years. Baseball players hustle for decades to perfect their craft. A chess master might spend a lifetime getting to the top. Luckily, you can pick up Duel Masters much faster than that, but you still must work hard to become a pro. In the following pages, we'll show you how to handle situations like a Kaijudo Master and turn your deck's trash pile into a treasure mound.

choosing a deck

BASIC TIP: Your deck should contain 40 cards and should be built around a victory condition or theme. For fun, you could build a deck that summoned only gel fish, or you may want to include only cards that speed along your victory condition.

ADVANCED TIP: Consider the metagame in your local area. Simply put, the metagame represents all the deck types being played and the frequency that each deck shows up. If 10 out of 40 people play a Fire speed deck at your next tournament, your deck better have cheap blockers or you'll get steamrolled. To be a serious contender, you must know all the dominant decks and prepare your deck accordingly.

mana zone

BASIC TIP: Play a card from your hand as mana each turn until you can cast anything in your deck. If your opening hand holds two or more cards from the same civilization, play one of them early to activate that color for the rest of the game.

ADVANCED TIP: When you reach your mana ceiling — the mana total that will cast your most expensive card — you have a decision to make. Should you continue playing mana so you can cast multiple cards in a turn, or should you hold back so you can play the extra creatures and spells against your opponent? Generally, you want the extra cards in your hand.

expert strategy

Battle Zone

BASIC TIP: Summon a creature a turn with a cost equal to the mana you have in play.

ADVANCED TIP: Hold some of your more powerful creature abilities for just the right time. You usually don't want to play Water's Corile and bounce your opponent's two-mana Bloody Squito. He'll simply replay it next turn without much setback. However, after your opponent plays Fire's Explosive Fighter Ucarn and destroys two of his mana cards, you definitely want to use Corile to make your opponent repeat that painful process.

SHIELD ZONE

BASIC TIP: Yes, you must destroy all your opponent's shields to win. No, you don't need to destroy them immediately. Each shield that you destroy gives your opponent one more card in hand, so if you can't finish him off, hold off on those last few attacks until you're properly set up.

ADVANCED TIP: Most decks will run between eight and 12 shield triggers. If you run eight, odds are that one of your shields will end up with a shield trigger (two shields if you run 16). Decks that rely on control spells like Terror Pit, Tornado Flame, and Spiral Gate may go as high as 16 to 20 shield triggers.

GRAVEYARD

BASIC TIP: Pack cards like Darkness' Dark Reversal and Nature's Thorny Mandra if you want to retrieve "dead" cards stuck in your graveyard. These cards can recycle some of your best cards and put them to good use again.

ADVANCED TIP: Graveyard tricks can get complicated, so be on the lookout for combos. For example, Fire's Artisan Picora can nuke a mana card into your graveyard, and Darkness' Amber Piercer can return it to your hand after it attacks.

attackers

BASIC TIP: Continue to destroy shields with your creatures so long as you can't be counterattacked. Once an enemy creature comes into play that can destroy your tapped creature, you must weigh whether it's worth losing the creature to destroy a shield.

ADVANCED TIP: Pay attention to creature abilities that trigger when they attack. Darkness' Horrid Worm forces your opponent to discard when it attacks, and Fire's Bolzard Dragon burns one of your opponent's mana cards. Not only are they powerful, but they go off before your creature becomes blocked, so they will happen no matter what!

BLOCKERS

BASIC TIP: Blockers provide your only form of consistent defense. Play cheap blockers early to stop speed attacks, and powerful blockers to stall all attackers.

ADVANCED TIP: Don't forget that your blockers can intercept an attack on one of your tapped creatures. If you want to save that tapped creature, throw your blocker into the combat instead.

expert strategy

evolution

BASIC TIP: Think of evolutions as creature upgrades. They are some of the most powerful creatures in the game, so play them if you can collect them.

ADVANCED TIP: Build your entire deck around the evolution. You always want to have a target for your evolution. The majority of your creatures should be the same creature race as your evolution, such as parasite worms for the Chaos Worm. Remember, your evolutions can attack immediately — they don't have summoning sickness!

SURVIVORS

BASIC TIP: In the latest set, Survivors of the Megapocalypse, creatures now have speed attacker and triple breaker. Speed attackers ignore summoning sickness, so consider them for any fast decks. Triple breaker only shows up in huge creatures — treat them as your main finisher in a creature-driven deck.

ADVANCED TIP: The set's namesake feature, survivors, adds a whole new dimension to the game. Survivors give their abilities to other survivors, so the more you have in play the more powerful they become. It's not worth playing with one or two — your whole deck should be devoted to them if you go that route.

CRASH COURSE: DARKNESS

Most of Darkness' creatures are blind, but they can still see you to victory. Armed with slayers and powerful destruction spells, the Darkness civilization starts off slow and builds up strength — until you're ready to strike!

TIP #1: THINK DEFENSE

Speed decks will take advantage of your expensive cards and destroy all your shields if you're not careful. To stop early charges, include cheap Darkness blockers like Bloody Squito and Wandering Braineater.

TIP #2: DESTRUCTION RULES

Budget Darkness decks should run four copies of the common destruction spell Death Smoke. If you can afford the rare Terror Pit, add four of those to control the battle zone even better.

TIP #3: BIG COSTS A LOT

f a card costs seven mana or more, it may be too expensive to play. Unless
your Darkness spells can control the battle zone, or you team up with Nature
to make mana quickly, your Vampire Silphy may have to sit on the sideline.

TIP #4: EVOLVE OR DIE

ournament decks rely on Evolution creatures because their abilities car
e such a bargain. Consider playing lots of parasite worms to evolve the
estructive Chaos Worm or giant Ultracide Worm.

TIP #5: DISCARD DOMINATION

orcing your opponent to lose cards through creatures (Horrid Worm) and
ells (Ghost Touch) can work, but only if you devote your whole deck to the
use. A few discard cards won't be enough to penalize your opponent

HOW TO BUILD A DARKNESS DECK

No two Darkness decks are the same, so stamp your personality on each of your creations. Whether it's a fun deck that calls forth only ghosts or a deck that pounds away with Deathliger, Lion of Chaos, you should be happy with the card mix and proud that you put together something that hangs with your friends' best decks.

OUR IDEA: First, decide on your deck's theme. Will it rush at your opponent as quickly as possible, or hold the fort with damaging spells? Our Darkness deck will rely on slayers, powerful creatures that always destroy enemy creatures, even if they lose.

A SECOND IDEA: The slayer Scratchclaw gets bigger for each Darkness creature in the battle zone. Now we have a second theme: Play lots of smaller creatures so Scratchclaw can grow to giant size in no time at all.

SLAYERS: Because they're common cards, we'll include Bone Assassin, The Ripper (which is a little expensive), and Wisp Howler, Shadow of Tears (which slays only Light and Nature creatures). We'll also add one copy of the rare Gigagiele and one uncommon Gigakail. The star of our deck, Scratchclaw, gets two copies, but only because it might be tough to find more. If you can collect four Scratchclaw cards, take out a Bone Assassin and Wisp Howler to fit the maximum.

HOW TO BUILD A DARKNESS DECK

CHEAP CREATURES: All your blockers cost two or less mana, including Marrow Ooze, The Twister, which is the only Darkness creature that costs one mana to play. On the offensive side, your 2000-power Writhing Bone Ghoul and 1000-power Bone Piercer cost two mana each. We want to play them quickly to help out Scratchclaw.

DESTRUCTION SPELLS: To back up our attackers, we have Death Smoke and Terror Pit to destroy enemy creatures. If you want, you can also run Critical Blade to remove enemy blockers and two more Terror Pits to help out on defense.

Darkness Deck: The Slayer Squad

Scratch and claw your way to victory, or should we say Scratchclaw to the finish line? Play as many Darkness creatures as you can, so when you big powerhouse creature, Scratchclaw, shows up, it will be huge! With 12 blockers and six destruction spells, you can hold out on defense until you et up your offense. Teamed up with your fellow slayers, Scratchclaw wil scare or destroy anyone in its path!

BLOCKERS

4 Bloody Squito (Base Set)

4 Marrow Ooze, The Twister (Evo-Crushinators of Doom)

4 Wandering Braineater (Base Set)

DESTRUCTION SPELLS

4 Death Smoke (Base Set)

2 Terror Pit (Base Set)

SLAYERS

1 Bone Assassin, The Ripper (Base Set)

1 Gigagiele (Base Set)

1 Gigakail (Survivors of the Megapocalypse)

2 Scratchclaw (Rampage of the Super Warriors)

4 Wailing Shadow Belbetphlo (Rampage of the Super Warriors)

4 Wisp Howler, Shadow of Tears (Survivors of the Megapocalypse)

MORE CREATURES

4 Bone Piercer (Rampage of the Super Warriors)

1 Trox, General of Destruction (Shadowclash of Blinding Night)

4 Writhing Bone Ghoul (Base Set)

Darkness Puzzle: Grave Doubts

HOW TO BEAT THE PUZZLE: By the end of the turn, you must have two blockers in hand to stop your opponent's attackers next turn. What do you do?

SETUP:

1. You have two shields, and your opponent has two creatures in play. If you can't slow his attackers down, he will win the following turn.
2. Your mana zone can produce five mana (all Darkness cards).
3. You currently have no cards in your graveyard.
4. You must race your opponent, so you want to destroy two of his shields this turn and play as many offensive creatures as you can.
5. It's your turn, but you have already drawn your card (Vampire Silphy).

IN YOUR HAND:

Black Feather, Shadow of Rage

Skeleton Thief, The Revealer

Stinger Worm

Vampire Silphy

IN PLAY (YOUR SIDE):

Amber Piercer

Marrow Ooze, The Twister

Wandering Braineater

IN PLAY (YOUR OPPONENT'S SIDE):

Chilias, The Oracle

Fear Fang

PUZZLE ANSWER:

1. Play Black Feather, Shadow of Rage, and sacrifice your Wandering Braineater.

2. Play Skeleton Thief, The Revealer, and return the Wandering Braineater (a living dead creature) to your hand.

3. Attack with Marrow Ooze, The Twister. It goes to the graveyard after the attack.

4. Attack with Amber Piercer. It returns the Marrow Ooze to your hand.

5. You now have two blockers in hand and you're ready to defend on your next turn.

When it's time for an inferno of destructive creatures and spells, build a Fire civilization deck. You will have lots of explosive choices, especially in the cheap creature department. Don't get burned by poor selections.

TIP #1: GO, GO!

Fire owns the game's quickest creatures, including one-mana attackers foreign to most other civilizations. Survivors of the Megapocalypse introduces speed attackers that ignore summoning sickness, so you can knock out shields right from the start.

TIP #2: NO BLOCKING

If you're Fire-only, forget about defense. There are no blockers. Devote your energy instead to attacking early and following up with a big finisher creature when you have more mana. Destruction spells serve as your defense.

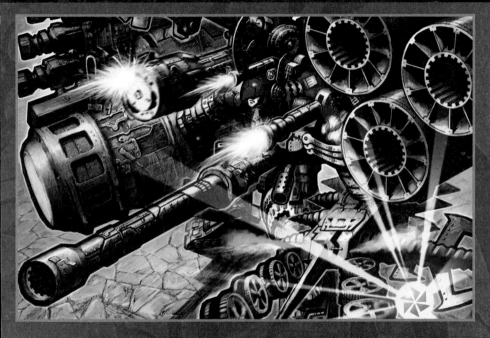

TIP #3: BURNING UP

In most Fire-heavy decks, play with Crimson Hammer, Tornado Flame, and Volcanic Arrows. These three destruction spells remove any threat of 6000-power or less. Avoid Burst Shot unless you aren't playing with cheap creatures.

TIP #4: SUPER EVOLVERS

Both human evolutions will power up the troops, but Armored Blaster Valdios earns the higher command rank over Armored Cannon Balbaro. The four-mana Valdios gains double breaker and a 6000-power body that's hard to kill.

TIP #5: MANA TOAST

Fire also specializes in mana destruction. When you want to deny your opponent resources, stock up on creatures like Bombersaur and Bolzard Dragon. For super mana destruction, team up with Nature and cast Cataclysmic Eruption.

HOW TO BUILD A FIRE DECK

When a rocket takes off from the launchpad, scientists count down to its blastoff. Well, with Fire decks, the fireworks begin almost immediately. A card like Crimson Hammer can destroy a creature as early as the second turn, and your creatures blast more than shields — some of them can destroy mana cards or other creatures!

OUR IDEA: Throw so much destruction into one deck that enemy creatures can't stay in the battle zone for more than a couple of turns. Once we have control, our Fire deck will cast some powerful finishers to whittle away all of our opponent's shields.

BACKUP CIVILIZATION: If we truly want destruction of epic proportions, we'll team Fire up with Darkness. Together, these two civilizations hold almost all of the anti-creature spells and provide enough firepower to scour the battle zone clean.

BOARD CONTROL: Start off by adding some Darkness blockers like Bloody Squito and Dark Clown. As for removal spells, take Fire's three best — Crimson Hammer, Tornado Flame, Volcanic Arrows — and add Darkness' two main destruction spells, Terror Pit and Death Smoke. That's 20 destruction spells, which will handle anything that shows its face. Because destruction is the deck's theme, include four copies of each if you can. Fill in with additional creatures for any rare card you might be missing.

HOW TO BUILD A FIRE DECK

MANA DESTRUCTION: Once we have control, our big creatures will play on the mana-destruction theme to keep our opponent from casting anything equally big. The rare Bolzard Dragon and Bombersaur can reduce an opponent's mana supply and prevent them from mounting a successful defense.

RARE POTENTIAL: With so many rares, try playing with four common Galsaurs. The rock beast becomes an 8000-power double breaker if it's the only creature. If you have the rares, four copies of the Bolzard Dragon will help you destroy your opponent's mana that much faster.

FIRE DECK: FIRE AND BRIMSTONE

Nothing lasts long under this destructive pressure. With five different destruction spells and one destructive creature (Rothus), enemy creatures can't even catch their breath, let alone attack. If an enemy evolution manages to slip through, throw a blocker in the way and gun it down with one of your spells next turn. When the threats die down, summon forth a Bolzard Dragon or Galsaur to limit your opponent's options, and life, to a few turns.

BLOCKERS

4 Bloody Squito (Base Set)

2 Dark Clown (Base Set)

2 Wandering Braineater (Base Set)

DESTRUCTION SPELLS

4 Crimson Hammer (Base Set)

4 Death Smoke (Base Set)

4 Terror Pit (Base Set)

4 Tornado Flame (Base Set)

4 Volcanic Arrows (Rampage of the Super Warriors)

MANA DESTRUCTION

2 Bolzard Dragon (Evo-Crushinators of Doom)

2 Bombersaur (Evo-Crushinators of Doom)

MORE CREATURES

2 Draglide (Base Set)

4 Galsaur (Evo-Crushinators of Doom)

2 Rothus, The Traveler (Base Set)

Fire Puzzle: no speed Limit

HOW TO BEAT THE PUZZLE: How many turns will it take you to beat your opponent? Play the cards in your hand out to the battle zone in the order that will destroy your opponent's shields the fastest.

SETUP:

1. Your opponent has five shields and has decided to cut you a break — he won't play any creatures for the first few turns.
2. Your mana zone can produce five mana (all Fire cards).
3. You can assume that each turn you draw a card and play it as more mana.
4. You have already drawn your card this turn and played it to your mana zone.
5. On the fourth turn, your opponent will play two blockers.

IN YOUR HAND:

Bombat, General of Speed

Armored Cannon Balbaro

Fatal Attacker Horvath

Fire Sweeper Burning Hellion

Rumble Gate

IN PLAY (YOUR SIDE):
None to start

IN PLAY (YOUR OPPONENT'S SIDE):
Dark Raven, Shadow of Grief
(on fourth turn)
Emerald Grass (on fourth turn)

PUZZLE ANSWER:

1. On the first turn, play Bombat, General of Speed, and attack (it's a speed attacker and doesn't have summoning sickness). Destroy the first shield.

2. On the second turn, play Fatal Attacker Horvath, then evolve Armored Cannon Balbaro from Horvath. Destroy the second and third shields with Bombat and Balbaro.

3. On the third turn, play Fire Sweeper Burning Hellion. Destroy the fourth and fifth shields with Bombat and Balbaro.

4. On the fourth turn, attack with all three creatures. Your opponent's blockers will stop two of them, but your third will slip through for the victory.

27

Some people like to diet on food light in calories. So do your opponent a favor and put him through a rigid diet regimen as he scrambles to block your Light attackers and races to avoid Light spells that will put his army on the next serving platter.

TIP #1: VANILLA WAFERS

A vanilla creature in Duel Masters is one without any special abilities. Light has a large number of creatures with good power-to-cost ratio, but nothing much else. When you want creature tricks, you might want to head to the Darkness or Water realms.

TIP #2: BEST BLOCKERS

While Water defends well, Light defends better. Light's blockers can't attack players, but they can go after tapped creatures and destroy the enemy before it gets back up to attack again. If you want defense and don't need a specific Water spell, step into the Light.

TIP #3: TAP DANCE

The ability to tap a creature might seem minor on the surface. After all, that creature just untaps and attacks the next turn, right? Maybe not. Cards like Moonlight Flash tap enemies, which you can then remove with your bigger creatures.

TIP #4: HUGE EVOLVERS

Light claims the world's biggest blocker in the 9500-power Ladia Bale, The Inspirational, which can also attack. Light's evolution might be slow, but you can stall with other guardian blockers and buy extra time for the big bang.

TIP #5: SEARCHLIGHT

No other civilization searches its deck better than Light, though it can fetch only spell cards. Turn to cards like Laguna, Lightning Enforcer; Logic Cube; and Rayla, Truth Enforce to pluck the perfect spell for the situation.

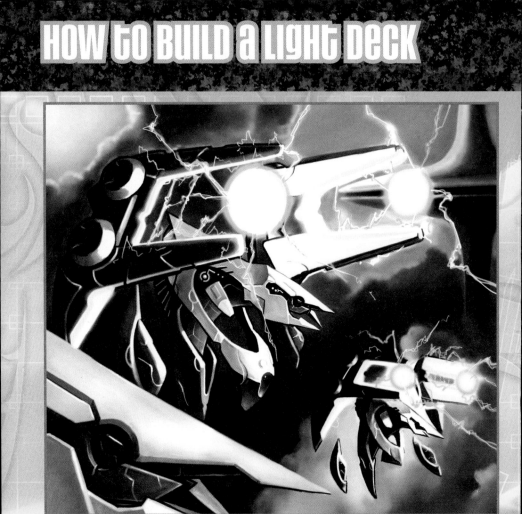

A little bit of this, a dab of that, mix it all together and Light comes up with something that will take other decks to the mat. By combining Light's spell searching with Nature's creature searching, this deck calls forth mammoth blockers and attackers to waste the opposition. If your opponent gets upset about your power deck, tell him to "lighten up."

OUR IDEA: Some of Light's power creatures like Ladia Bale, The Inspirational and Hanusa, Radiance Elemental can erase the Darkness and overpower Fire's puny flickers. The deck wants to stall while it sets up for the big play.

SECOND IDEA: We'll add Nature for some mana acceleration to help reach our big boys faster. With access to both Light and Nature shield triggers, we can play Logic Cube to search for spells and Dimension Gate to search for creatures.

DEFENSE: We have to stay alive long enough to pull off our tricks, so that means blockers. Starting with four of the one-mana La Ura Giga, Sky Guardian blockers, we can add the two-mana Emerald Grass and three-mana Senatine Jade Tree. With a mana curve like this, we can drop a blocker on the first three turns if we need the defense.

BIG BOYS: Both Ladia Bale and Hanusa crush opponents with their 9500-power bodies. Aeris, Flight Elemental can absolutely destroy a Darkness deck, since it attacks untapped Darkness creatures with a 9000 power. Search it out with Dimension Gate against Darkness opponents; otherwise, play it for mana. The mega-powerful Urth, Purifying Elemental strikes as a 6000-power, double-breaker attacker, then untaps so your opponent can never attack it without some combat tricks.

RARE POTENTIAL: Your large finisher creatures are interchangeable. Since many are rare or super rare and tough to collect, add whatever big creatures you have to fill in for missing teammates.

LIGHT DECK: BIG BOMBS

Start off like a deceptive snail and play creatures that give you extra mana and blockers. While your opponent might not think much of your force early on, wait until you have six mana and suddenly the lightbulb will wink on above his head. Tap annoying enemies with Holy Awe and Moonlight Flash, then destroy them with your blockers. If your big boys stick around, it's lights-out for your opponent in record time.

BLOCKERS
2 Emerald Grass (Base Set)
2 Senatine Jade Tree (Base Set)
4 La Ura Giga, Sky Guardian (Base Set)
1 Ladia Bale, The Inspirational (Evo-Crushinators of Doom)

MANA ACCELERATION
4 Bronze-Arm Tribe (Base Set)
4 Silver Axe (Evo-Crushinators of Doom)

SEARCH CARDS
4 Dimension Gate (Base Set)
4 Logic Cube (Evo-Crushinators of Doom)

OTHER CARDS
1 Aeris, Flight Elemental (Shadowclash of Blinding Night)
1 Hanusa, Radiance Elemental (Base Set)
2 Holy Awe (Base Set)
2 Lah, Purification Elemental (Base Set)
4 Magris, Vizier of Magnetism (Evo-Crushinators of Doom)
2 Moonlight Flash (Base Set)
2 Natural Snare (Base Set)
1 Urth, Purifying Elemental (Base Set)

HOW TO BEAT THE PUZZLE: How many shields can you finish with at the end of the turn?

SETUP:

1. You currently have five shields, but your opponent must be building up for something big. Add to your shields for some extra defense.
2. Your opponent has no shields.
3. Your mana zone can produce 10 mana (all Light cards).
4. One of the cards in your mana zone is Sundrop Armor. When you cast Sundrop Armor, you add a card from your hand to your shield zone facedown.
5. You have already drawn your card this turn (Dia Nork).

IN YOUR HAND:

Aless, The Oracle

Boomerang Comet

Dia Nork, Moonlight Guardian

IN PLAY (YOUR SIDE):

Aless, The Oracle

Raza Vega, Thunder Guardian

Szubs Kin, Twilight Guardian

IN PLAY (YOUR OPPONENT'S SIDE):

Chilias, The Oracle

Fear Fang

PUZZLE ANSWER:

1. Cast Boomerang Comet and replace Sundrop Armor in your mana zone with Boomerang Comet.
2. Play Sundrop Armor and add either of the two remaining cards in your hand to your shield zone for six shields.
3. Attack with Aless, The Oracle. Your opponent must block it or lose the game. When Aless "dies," add it to your shield zone.
4. Attack with Raza Vega, Thunder Guardian. Your opponent must block it or lose the game. When Raza Vega "dies," add it to your shield zone. You now have eight shields in play.

Nature knows how to grow its creatures to crazy sizes. With lots of mana acceleration, the Nature civilization plays out its more expensive creatures (and spells) faster than its competitors. After seeing your deck just once, your opponent will turn green with envy.

TIP #1: MANA MAKERS

Almost every Nature deck benefits from Bronze-Arm Tribe and Silver Axe, which provide extra mana cards early in the game. If you can fit it, the underestimated Mighty Shouter gives you an extra mana boost when it dies.

TIP #2: BLOCKER-LESS DEFENDERS

Nature has no blockers. Even so, it's not helpless to stop attacks. Creatures like Steel Smasher and Poisonous Dahlia might not attack players, but their big bodies are cheap for the price and can crush tapped creatures.

TIP #3: SUPER STUDS

Don't let the mana cost fool you. With Nature's fast mana, treat a seven-mana Xeno Mantis as if it were six or maybe even five mana. Even the nine-mana Fortress Shell isn't out of range. Your deck will soar up to these levels quickly.

TIP #4: SPEEDY EVOLVERS

Believe it or not, Nature, not Fire, has the fastest evolution. Barkwhip, The Smasher costs only two mana and transforms one of your beast folk into a 5000-power world-beater. Fighter Dual Fang is no slouch at six mana, either.

TIP #5: ADDED DIMENSION

Where Light searches for spells, Nature fetches creatures. Dimension Gate and Rumbling Terahorn can find exactly the creatures you need. This gives you the flexibility to play one copy of certain creatures and still reliably draw them.

HOW TO BUILD A NATURE DECK

Nature can bloom mana to the moon, and it can also take it all away. As this deck plops down more and more mana, it summons fierce attackers and ramps up to a huge spell that will deny your opponent his mana. After you're through with him, your opponent might be lucky to play a lowly Deadly Fighter Braid Claw or Writhing Bone Ghoul.

OUR IDEA: Deny an opponent the resources he needs to play his strongest creatures and spells. If we can pull that off, our strongest creatures will take home the prize.

SECOND IDEA: Arguably, Nature has the best evolutions. Why not take advantage of them in a deck heavy on beast folk that produce extra mana for the deck? Once the beast folk serve their primary purpose, transform them into deadly attackers.

HEAVENLY MANA: Start with four uncommon Poisonous Mushroom cards. These cost you a card out of your hand to produce an extra mana, but it's worth it in this deck where mana speed is essential. At three mana, include four copies of Bronze-Arm Tribe (the best mana-producer), Silver Axe and Mighty Shouter. If you need the extra mana, you should suicide the Silver Axe or Mighty Shouter into enemy blockers.

MANA NO MORE: The faster you get up to eight mana, the quicker victory will come on your side. Even though Cataclysmic Eruption is a rare, include four. This deck can climb up to the eight-mana mark quickly, and you must have a Cataclysmic Eruption in your hand when you hit that threshold. Of course, four copies of Mana Crisis will help slow down your opponent by destroying a single mana card on the opposing side.

DESPERATION DESTRUCTION:

To up your Fire card count so that you have at least one Fire card to play as mana, we want eight Fire spells that aren't Cataclysmic Eruption (that's too valuable to use as mana unless you have two in your hand). The two best are Tornado Flame and Volcanic Arrows — they both destroy big creatures that could cause you serious problems.

nature deck: mana denied

You have no blockers. You have only eight spells to remove creatures. So what's all this about? Mana elimination. Speed your deck up to eight mana and you will devastate your opponent's mana supply with a single Cataclysmic Eruption spell. While your opponent tries to build mana back up, call out your finishers like the 5000-power Barkwhip, The Smasher, or the 6000-power Three-Eyed Dragonfly to deny your opponent the win.

MANA CREATURES

4 Bronze-Arm Tribe (Base Set)

4 Mighty Shouter (Base Set)

4 Poisonous Mushroom (Base Set)

4 Silver Axe (Evo-Crushinators of Doom)

MANA DESTRUCTION

4 Cataclysmic Eruption (Survivors of the Megapocalypse)

4 Mana Crisis (Evo-Crushinators of Doom)

REMOVAL SPELLS

4 Tornado Flame (Base Set)

4 Volcanic Arrows (Rampage of the Super Warriors)

FINISHERS

4 Barkwhip, The Smasher (Evo-Crushinators of Doom)

1 Fighter Dual Fang (Evo-Crushinators of Doom)

3 Three-Eyed Dragonfly (Shadowclash of Blinding Night)

nature puzzle: giant mana

HOW TO BEAT THE PUZZLE: Gain enough mana to cast the Ancient Giant on your next turn.

SETUP:

1. You won't be able to cast the Ancient Giant this turn, but just wait until next turn.
2. Your opponent has all his shields.
3. Your mana zone can produce four mana (all Nature cards).
4. You have already drawn your card this turn (Rumble Gate).

IN YOUR HAND:
Ancient Giant
Rainbow Stone
Rumble Gate

IN PLAY (YOUR SIDE):

Psyshroom

Silver Fist

Xeno Mantis

IN PLAY (YOUR OPPONENT'S SIDE):

No cards

PUZZLE ANSWER:

1. You begin with four mana.
2. Play Rumble Gate to your mana zone. (five mana)
3. Play Rainbow Stone and pull any card out of your deck to go to the mana zone. (six mana)
4. Attack with the Psyshroom and move the Rainbow Stone card in your graveyard to the mana zone.
   (seven mana)
5. Draw a card on your next turn and play it for mana. You now have the eight mana you need to summon
   forth the mighty Ancient Giant.

CRASH COURSE: WATER

Water might quench thirst in our world, but in Duel Masters it can choke the life out of your opponent. With cards that bounce your opponent's creatures out of the battle zone or draw lots of cards for your hand, the Water Civilization can answer any call.

TIP #1: TEMPORARY DESTRUCTION

Cards like Spiral Gate, Stained Glass, and Unicorn Fish can all remove a creature from the battle zone. Unlike most civilizations, Water has a ton of removal, but just remember it's temporary — your opponent can replay the creature next turn.

TIP #2: MAD CARDS

You may be attracted to Water for its ability to earn you lots of extra cards. Whenever building decks, consider cards like Astral Warper, Brain Serum, and Thought Probe. If you can make them work, your deck will become much quicker.

TIP #3: BLOCKING POWER

Light has better blockers, because Water's blockers can't attack other creatures. However, starting with the one-mana Marine Flower, Water's blockers slow down speed decks the best.

TIP #4: UNDERWATER SIEGE

Many Water creatures, like Candy Drop and Faerie Child, swim past your opponent's defenses because they can't be blocked. They can be attacked the following turn, so play with blockers to stop the counterattack.

TIP #5: WACKY WEAPONS

Looking for a weird or fun theme to throw off your friends? Try the Water Civilization, with cards like Recon Operation, which looks at your opponent's shields, and Divine Riptide that forces players to return all cards from the mana zone to their hands.

HOW TO BUILD A WATER DECK

Water creatures are slippery as eels. They like to win with a special ability that allows them to slip through the enemy defenses without being blocked. As the opposing shields pop one by one, the Water Civilization controls the battle zone with "bounce" spells that return creatures to their owners' hands. In our new deck, some of the Water abilities will be transferred to three other civilizations!

OUR IDEA: What's this deck's theme? Sharing. It's always a good idea to share with your brothers and sisters, and now that good-heartedness will pay off in a powerful Duel Masters deck. The survivor creatures from the Survivors of the Megapocalypse set give each other their abilities. Together they can become a fearsome force.

SURVIVORS: Only one survivor is a rare card, Darkness' Skullsweeper, so we'll include only two of those. The Smash Horn, your most essential survivor, gives all your creatures +1000 power, and they can grow to gigantic size if you manage more than one Smash Horn in the battle zone at once! To make sure you have enough cards to get the correct mana for a deck with four different civilizations, we'll include three or four copies of all the other survivors. Your Water survivors will provide the finishing touches. The Split-Head Hydroturtle gives you an extra card each time one of your survivors attacks — for even more options! — and the Spikestrike Ichthys proves deadly when it prevents any of your creatures from being blocked.

HOW TO BUILD A WATER DECK

BOUNCE SPELLS: We want four copies of Spiral Gate, which bounces one creature, and two copies of the more expensive Teleportation, which bounces two creatures. Play these spells on your opponent's attacking creatures to slow them down to a crawl.

OTHER SPELLS: Death Smoke will destroy big threats if you play it the turn after the creature enters the battle zone. You want four of those. You also need four Dimension Gate spells. You might end up casting it for free if it goes off as a shield trigger. If not, three mana to retrieve any survivor from your deck can be the answer to your prayers.

Water Deck: Survivors of the fittest

You've probably heard the saying "strength in numbers." Well, the survivors bring new meaning to that phrase. Play as many survivors as you can to rack up the special abilities, especially creatures like the Smash Horn that give all your survivors +1000 power. If you need defense, drop a Gallia Zohl, Iron Guardian (survivors become blockers). Your Water spells should slow down your opponent long enough to play your winning survivor — the Spikestrike Ichthys, who makes all your survivors unblockable!

BOUNCE SPELLS

4 Spiral Gate (Base Set)

2 Teleportation (Base Set)

MORE SPELLS

4 Death Smoke (Base Set)

4 Dimension Gate (Base Set)

SURVIVORS

2 Balloonshroom (Survivors of the Megapocalypse)

3 Ballus, Dogfight Enforcer (Survivors of the Megapocalypse)

4 Gallia Zohl, Iron Guardian (Survivors of the Megapocalypse)

3 Gigaling (Survivors of the Megapocalypse)

2 Skullsweeper (Survivors of the Megapocalypse)

4 Smash Horn (Survivors of the Megapocalypse)

4 Spikestrike Ichthys (Survivors of the Megapocalypse)

4 Split-Head Hydroturtle (Survivors of the Megapocalypse)

HOW TO BEAT THE PUZZLE: Draw through the rest of the cards in your deck this turn. Why? Because it's fun!

SETUP:

1. Your opponent decides to take a nap while your turn lasts half an hour.
2. Your mana zone can produce 11 mana (two Nature cards, nine Water cards).
3. You can attack if you like — your opponent doesn't have any blockers or shield triggers. He has five shields left.
4. You have already drawn your initial card this turn (Spiral Gate).

IN PLAY (YOUR SIDE):

Chaos Fish

Elf-X

Hypersquid Walter

Illusionary Merfolk

7 — Chaos Fish — EEL FISH
- This creature gets +1000 power for each other water creature you have in the battle zone.
- Whenever this creature attacks, you may draw a card for each of your other water creatures in the battle zone.

1000+

4 — Elf-X — TREE FOLK
- Your creatures each cost 1 less to summon. They can't cost less than 1.

The first Chimera to invade the Fiend Woods didn't expect an attack from the forest itself.

2000

3 — Hypersquid Walter — CYBER LORD
- Whenever this creature attacks, you may draw a card.

Using the twelve forbidden programs, the Cyber Lords created the elite Liquid People assault troops.

1000

5 — Illusionary Merfolk — EEL FISH
- When you put this creature into the battle zone, if you have a Cyber Lord in the battle zone, draw up to 3 cards.

The Cyber Lords' devotion to beauty is so extreme, they even designed their warrior race to have a pleasant appearance.

4000

IN YOUR HAND:

Revolver Fish

Spiral Gate

Tri-Horn Shepherd

CARDS IN YOUR DECK (IN ORDER FROM TOP TO BOTTOM):

Hunter Fish

Marine Flower

Aqua Hulcus

Aqua Vehicle

Stampeding Longhorn

Brain Serum

Golden Wing Striker

Aqua Knight

Red-Eye Scorpion

Faerie Child

Crystal Memory

PUZZLE ANSWER:

1. Play Spiral Gate and return Illusionary Merfolk to your hand. Replay Illusionary Merfolk for four mana. Remember: Elf-X is in play, so all your creatures cost one less.

2. Draw three cards from the Illusionary Merfolk since Hypersquid Walter is a cyber lord.

3. Play the three cards you drew — Hunter Fish, Marine Flower, Aqua Hulcus — for a total of four mana. When you play Aqua Hulcus, you draw one more card: Aqua Vehicle. Play this to use up the last of your mana.

4. Attack with Hypersquid Walter and draw a card.

5. Attack with Chaos Fish and draw six extra cards (one for each Water creature in the battle zone other than Chaos Fish). Congratulations, you have drawn 11 cards in one turn!

51

POWER TIPS

You probably haven't played in an official Duel Masters tournament. That's okay. Grab your card binder or complete checklist, and guess what — you have the same cards that the pros use! These are some of the more popular cards that you'll spot in tournament decks.

Darkness

BEST CREATURE: Chaos Worm
This evolution plays best over the smaller Horrid Worm. Use the Horrid Worm's discard ability as long as you can before morphing into the Chaos Worm's destruction mode.

BEST SPELL: Terror Pit
Obviously, you want the Terror Pit to go off for free as a shield trigger. If it ends up in your hand, hold it for an enemy that can't be destroyed by your other removal spells.

Fire

BEST CREATURE: Armored Blaster Valdios
Hit early with humans like Brawler Zyler or Mini Titan Gett, then when the defense builds up, transform one of them into Valdios and increase everyone by +1000 power.

BEST SPELL: Tornado Flame
When a shield trigger goes off, you don't have to use it. If there's no dangerous creature in play, draw Tornado Flame into your hand and wait for a better target.

BEST CREATURE: Ladia Bale, The Inspirational
Control the battle zone with lots of inspiration and brute force. The huge Ladia Bale blocks until all your defenses are set, then turns around and hits with the best of them.

BEST SPELL: Holy Awe
It's a one-card combo all by itself. When your opponent triggers it while attacking a shield, Holy Awe taps all enemy creatures and opens the door for a furious counterattack.

BEST CREATURE: Barkwhip, The Smasher
Any beast folk will do to morph into the super-fast, super-strong Barkwhip, The Smasher evolution, but the Bronze-Arm Tribe produces an extra mana before it transforms.

BEST SPELL: Natural Snare
Nature's only true destruction spell, this shield trigger works similar to Terror Pit. Don't worry that it gives your opponent extra mana — it's worth taking out his best creature.

BEST CREATURE: Corile
Target an evolution with this cyber lord, and your opponent loses two card draws as both the evolution and the card beneath it return to the top of your opponent's deck.

BEST SPELL: Brain Serum
More cards means more chances to draw your powerful creatures and spells. Brain Serum gives you two more chances, and it's free if it kicks off as a shield trigger.

tournament roundup

How many opponents will your deck slay? Sure, you might stomp your friends while you sit around the table one game night, but until you test the serious tournament waters and play against a variety of decks and opponents, you'll never know the true extent of your Duel Masters skills. Plus, don't you get tired of playing the same Fire deck your friend likes to break out?

When you want to try your hand at a fun and challenging experience, head to your local game store and see if they run JDC tournaments. A JDC tournament is a fun and rewarding league, where you can play similar-skilled players over the course of several weeks that comprise a season. Not only is it a blast, but you earn a foil Armored Groblav promo card (not available in any actual set) just for signing up. Finish near the top, and you gain the ultimate prize — a foil Barkwhip, The Smasher evolution card!

And that's not all. Whenever a new set releases, look for the prerelease tournaments that give you a sneak peek at the cards before they're on sale.

If your local game store doesn't run these tournaments, check out duelmasters.com, Wizards of the Coast's very own Web site that gives you the full skinny on everything Duel Masters, including a complete list of stores hosting various tournaments.

TOURNAMENT DECK #1: BARKWHIP BASHERS

You thought Fire had the speed creatures? Well, it does, and a human-based Fire deck can be as speedy as a gazelle with a lion nipping at its heels. However, Fire doesn't have Barkwhip, The Smasher. The cheapest evolution becomes the fastest big creature in the game when combined with a host of beast folk targets. Oh, yeah . . . Barkwhip, when tapped, gives all your beast folk +2000 power — which just happens to be 15 other creatures!

OUR IDEA: Ditch the defense and build a deck that can destroy your opponent almost before he gets his shields straightened. With Barkwhip, The Smasher and his beast folk comrades, there's very little room left for clunky things like blockers or destruction spells.

BEAST SPEED: You always want a target for Barkwhip on the third turn, the earliest that you can play him. Therefore, you want at least eight beast folk that cost two mana to make your friend Barkwhip really happy. Burning Mane and Torcon fit the bill nicely. Torcon is even one of those rare shield trigger creatures from Shadowclash of Blinding Night that might come in for free to help your offensive charge. Steel Smasher can work, too, but since it can't attack on its own, it really helps only to slow down your opponent's deck and not speed up yours (unless you evolve it with Barkwhip). At three mana, Bronze-Arm Tribe and Mighty Shouter enter as beast folk and provide extra mana in one way or another.

BIG ASSAULT: By the fourth or fifth turn, you'll want a large creature to pick up the pressure where your little guys left off. The super-rare Earthstomp Giant will prove spectacular if you can collect four copies for your deck. At 8000-power and double breaker, you can't stop this thing once it gets stomping!

THE BEST DEFENSE: You know what they say, "The best defense is a good offense." This deck takes it to heart with spells like Dimension Gate (to grab more creatures from your deck) and Aura Blast (to pump up your creatures for the final attack). Only one removal spell, Natural Snare, stays in the deck, not so much to wipe out an attacker but to destroy a troublesome blocker in your way.

TOURNAMENT DECK LIST: BARKWHIP BASHERS

No one can stop you if you run fast enough. While Barkwhip smashes through enemy defenses, accumulate mana to cast the mighty Earthstomp Giant. When the Giant attacks, it returns all creature cards in your mana zone to your hand. Normally, this could be a problem, but you can replay creatures quickly, especially the one-mana Sniper Mosquito cards. Suddenly, you have a gigantic army that will swarm worse than an angry beehive.

BEAST FOLK

4 Barkwhip, The Smasher (Evo-Crushinators of Doom)

4 Bronze-Arm Tribe (Base Set)

4 Burning Mane (Base Set)

4 Mighty Shouter (Base Set)

4 Torcon (Shadowclash of Blinding Night)

MORE CREATURES

4 Earthstomp Giant (Rampage of the Super Warriors)

4 Sniper Mosquito (Rampage of the Super Warriors)

YOUR SPELLS

4 Aura Blast (Base Set)

4 Dimension Gate (Base Set)

4 Natural Snare (Base Set)

Like a heavyweight boxer, this deck can take a pounding and dish it right back out. Three out of four cards in the deck have a control element to them, whether it's a creature like Corile that bounces an enemy creature from the battle zone or a defensive spell like Terror Pit that permanently deals with the threat. With extra card drawing, you can build up a strong hand and come out swinging when you're ready for the knockout punch.

OUR IDEA: Combine the power of card drawing with destruction. Naturally, this means we want to tap into the strengths of the Water and Darkness civilizations, and join the two into a removal machine.

CARD DRAWING:

Illusionary Merfolk draws you three extra cards if you have a cyber lord in play, so the deck runs eight cyber lords to try and pull off this great combo. Four Emeral cards allow you to swap a card in your hand for a shield, so you can set up a shield trigger or ditch something that won't be useful until later in the game for something that might have immediate effects. Corile, the best Water creature, returns a creature from play to the top of your opponent's deck, forcing him to redraw the same card on his next turn. Of course, you want to run the maximum four copies of Corile and Emeral — if you drop a single Illusionary Merfolk into play, you'll be happy, so three copies will do just fine.

CONTROL: When relying on Darkness, you should always play four Terror Pit spells, a complement of its good blockers if you need extra defense (Bloody Squito and Dark Clown), and, if you have room, the Chaos Worm for its destructive and aggressive power. To evolve the Chaos Worm, you need parasite worm targets, so that's why we've chosen four Horrid Worms and three Gregorian Worms as early creatures.

THE UPPERCUT: When you have an Illusionary Merfolk or Chaos Worm in the battle zone, start attacking your opponent's shields. Something big could get in the way, so you should stock up on Water's bounce spells like Spiral Gate and Teleportation. Paired with Darkness' destruction, the one-two combination puts opponents down for the count.

TOURNAMENT DECK LIST: BLACK AND BRUISE

Start out with an early Emeral to set up your shields or a Bloody Squito if you need a blocker against a quick deck. Use your control spells to stall your opponent or obliterate his creatures. When you reach the five-mana mark, you can go for the kill with the Chaos Worm or draw lots of cards with Illusionary Merfolk. An evolution bothering you? Play Corile and send both enemy cards to the top of your opponent's deck. Now, that's better than a punch to the ol' kisser.

ATTACKING CREATURES

4 Chaos Worm (Evo-Crushinators of Doom)

3 Gregorian Worm (Shadowclash of Blinding Night)

4 Horrid Worm (Evo-Crushinators of Doom)

CARD MANIPULATION

4 Corile (Evo-Crushinators of Doom)

4 Emeral (Rampage of the Super Warriors)

3 Illusionary Merfolk (Base Set)

CONTROL SPELLS

4 Spiral Gate (Base Set)

3 Teleportation (Base Set)

4 Terror Pit (Base Set)

BLOCKERS

4 Bloody Squito (Base Set)

3 Dark Clown (Base Set)

63

CLASH OF THE TITANS!

Absolute Darkness meets ultimate Light in a "blinding night" that threatens to tear the five civilizations apart. In the war that rips through Duel Masters' fourth set, the civilizations take sides. Fire allies with Darkness, Nature helps out Light, while Water remains neutral, working well with everyone.

Enter a world of new surprises and super-powerful creatures to fuel up your Duel Masters decks. From creatures that come into play for free to evolutions for the high-powered races, the civilizations gain more weapons than ever in this set, especially Darkness and Light, which have more cards than the other civilizations!

This expansion set contains 60 cards:
5 super rare ✢
5 very rare ✪
15 rare ★
15 uncommon ✦
20 common ●

Flip through the next seven pages for your first look at **Shadowclash of Blinding Night!**

Ballom, Master of Death
DEMON COMMAND
8

EVOLUTION CREATURE

- Evolution—Put on one of your Demon Commands.
- When you put this creature into the battle zone, destroy all creatures except darkness creatures.
- Double breaker *(This creature breaks 2 shields.)*

"You see a world. I see a graveyard-to-be."

12000

Chains of Sacrifice
8

SPELL

- Destroy up to 2 of your opponent's creatures.
- Destroy one of your creatures.

"The only thing stronger than my chains is fear."
—Inas, General of Destruction

Darkpact
2

SPELL

- Put any number of cards from your mana zone into your graveyard. Then draw that many cards.

"Why isn't mortals embrace despair? All my ghoul friends really seem to enjoy it."
—Ballom, Master of Death

Gigabolver
CHIMERA
4

CREATURE

- Players can't use the "shield trigger" abilities of light cards.

It looks like a hideous monster, but there's really a sweet little girl deep down inside. To its stomach.

3000

Gregoria, Princess of War
DARK LORD
6

CREATURE

- Each Demon Command in the battle zone gets +2000 power and has "blocker." *(Whenever one of your opponent's creatures attacks, you may tap a creature that has "blocker" to stop the attack. Then the 2 creatures battle.)*

"Three fools in the clouds had better learn to like eternal majesty!"

5000

Gregorian Worm
PARASITE WORM
4

CREATURE

- Shield trigger *(When this creature is put into your hand from your shield zone, you may summon it immediately for no cost.)*

To a Gregorian worm, the world falls into two categories: things it can eat, and ... Well, so far there's just the one category.

3000

Locomotiver
HEDRIAN
4

CREATURE

- Shield trigger *(When this creature is put into your hand from your shield zone, you may summon it immediately for no cost.)*
- When you put this creature into the battle zone, your opponent discards a card at random from his hand.

If you think that's scary, you should see the coboose.

1000

Mongrel Man
HEDRIAN
5

CREATURE

- Whenever another creature is destroyed, you may draw a card.

"Shut off a light for a split second, and darkness rushes in to fill the void. That should be an easy war."

2000

Photocide, Lord of the Wastes
DEMON COMMAND
5

CREATURE

- This creature can't attack players.
- This creature can attack untapped light creatures.

"I will snuff out the sun and the stars! Then it's over to the candles and the lanterns. If I have time, I'll take care of those glow sticks people wear around their necks. But the sun is first!"

9000

Purple Piercer
BRAIN JACKER
3

CREATURE

- This creature can't be attacked by light creatures.
- This creature can't be blocked by light creatures.

You do not want to get into a tickle fight with this thing.

2000

Shadow Moon, Cursed Shade
GHOST
3

CREATURE

- Each other darkness creature in the battle zone gets +2000 power.

It spins a web of evil spells, all for its mistress, the Princess of War.

3000

Skeleton Thief, the Revealer
LIVING DEAD
4

CREATURE

- When you put this creature into the battle zone, you may return a Living Dead from your graveyard to your hand.

"I've dug up a pelvis, five kneecaps, and a bucketful of ribs tonight. But I still can't find any hands!"

2000

Soul Gulp
4

SPELL

• Your opponent chooses and discards a card from his hand for each light creature he has in the battle zone.

The first victim of the war between light and dark was the sky.

Trox, General of Destruction
7

DEMON COMMAND

• When you put this creature into the battle zone, your opponent discards a card at random from his hand for each other darkness creature you have in the battle zone.
• Double breaker *(This creature breaks 2 shields.)*

"Say goodbye to the daytime."

9000

Volcano Smog, Deceptive Shade
6

GHOST

• Each light creature costs 2 more to summon, and each light spell costs 2 more to cast.

"Is there any word more meaningless than 'hope'? Besides 'Starforgiveness,' of course."

5000

★

Aeris, Flight Elemental
ANGEL COMMAND

CREATURE

- This creature can't attack players.
- This creature can attack untapped darkness creatures.

"All armies, move out! It's time to make Photocide see the light!"

9000

Alcadeias, Lord of Spirits
ANGEL COMMAND

EVOLUTION CREATURE

- Evolution—Put on one of your Angel Commands.
- Double breaker (This creature breaks 2 shields.)
- Players can't cast spells other than light spells.

"We have watched and we have waited. Now we act."

12500

Amber Grass
STARLIGHT TREE

CREATURE

◇ Shield trigger (When this creature is put into your hand from your shield zone, you may summon it immediately for no cost.)

Each surge of electricity triggers a growth spurt.

3000

Fu Reil, Seeker of Storms
MECHA THUNDER

CREATURE

- Players can't use the "shield trigger" abilities of darkness cards.

"The only smoke screen coming from Ballom will be the one billowing off of his smoldering carcass."

5000

Full Defensor
SPELL

- ◇ Shield trigger (When this spell is put into your hand from your shield zone, you may cast it immediately for no cost.)
- Until the start of your next turn, each of your creatures in the battle zone gets "Blocker (Whenever an opponent's creature attacks, you may tap this creature to stop the attack. Then the 2 creatures battle.)"

Gulan Rias, Speed Guardian
GUARDIAN

CREATURE

- This creature can't be attacked by darkness creatures.
- This creature can't be blocked by darkness creatures.

It outraces shooting stars.

2000

Kolon, the Oracle
LIGHT BRINGER

CREATURE

- ◇ Shield trigger (When this creature is put into your hand from your shield zone, you may summon it immediately for no cost.)
- When you put this creature into the battle zone, you may choose one of your opponent's creatures in the battle zone and tap it.

1000

Milieus, the Daystretcher
BERSERKER

CREATURE

- ▢ Blocker (Whenever an opponent's creature attacks, you may tap this creature to stop the attack. Then the 2 creatures battle.)
- Each darkness creature costs 2 more to summon, and each darkness spell costs 2 more to cast.

2500

Mist Rias, Sonic Guardian
GUARDIAN

CREATURE

- Whenever another creature is put into the battle zone, you may draw a card.

"When you shine a light into a dark corner, the shadow instantly vanishes. This should be an easy war."

2000

Ouks, Vizier of Restoration
INITIATE

CREATURE

- When this creature would be destroyed, add it to your shields face down instead.

"Laser web"? Check. "Laser spider"? Still no order.

1000

Re Bil, Seeker of Archery
MECHA THUNDER

CREATURE

- Each other light creature in the battle zone gets +2000 power.
- Double breaker (This creature breaks 2 shields.)

Bull's-eye!

6000

Rimuel, Cloudbreak Elemental
ANGEL COMMAND

CREATURE

- When you put this creature into the battle zone, tap one of your opponent's creatures in the battle zone for each untapped light card in your mana zone.
- Double breaker (This creature breaks 2 shields.)

"As the sun streams through Blindingo, so shall some other poetic stuff happen."

6000

Ancient Giant — 8 — GIANT
- This creature can't be blocked by darkness natures.
- Double breaker (This creature breaks 2 shields.)

"I don't care how hugely, massively, gigantically big it is! Slap it before it gets to General Peace."
—Zagloon, Knight of Darkness

9000

Cannon Shell — 4 — COLONY BEETLE
- Shield trigger (When this creature is put into your hand from your shield zone, you may summon it immediately for no cost.)
- This creature gets +1000 power for each shield you have.

It has hungered for revenge since the Dark Lords invaded.

1000+

Dew Mushroom — 3 — BALLOON MUSHROOM
- Each darkness creature costs 1 more to summon, and each darkness spell costs 1 more to cast.

"The only thing grosser than eating a mushroom is having a mushroom eat me."
—Glism the Tormentor

1000

Exploding Cactus — 3 — TREE FOLK
- While you have a light creature in the battle zone, this creature gets +2000 power.

"Eww! Now that's disgusting!" —Mongrel Man

2000+

Mystic Inscription — 6 — SPELL
- Add the top card of your deck to your shields face down.

"The Angel Command have sent us a divine message! Let's see: 'Ice cream, rye bread, bananas, laundry detergent'..."

Niofa, Horned Protector — 6 — HORNED BEAST
- Evolution—Put on one of your Horned Beasts.
- When you put this creature into the battle zone, search your deck. You may take a nature creature from your deck, show that creature to your opponent, and put it into your hand. Then shuffle your deck.
- Double breaker (This creature breaks 2 shields.)

9000

Supporting Tulip — 5 — TREE FOLK
- Each Angel Command in the battle zone has "power attacker +4000." (While attacking, a creature that has "power attacker +4000" gets +4000 power.)

They only bloom in outer space.

4000

Sword of Benevolent Life — 2 — SPELL
- Each of your creatures in the battle zone gets +1000 power until the end of the turn for each light creature you have in the battle zone.

"Absolute has given us a great gift! We're saved! We're... umm, can anyone lift that thing?" —Fear Fang

Three-Eyed Dragonfly — 5 — GIANT INSECT
- Whenever this creature attacks, you may destroy one of your other creatures. If you do, this creature gets +2000 power and has "double breaker" until the end of the turn. (A creature that has "double breaker" breaks 2 shields.)

The third eye sees a few seconds into the future.

4000+

Torcon — 2 — BEAST FOLK
- Shield trigger (When this creature is put into your hand from your shield zone, you may summon it immediately for no cost.)

"This ritual seeds the sky with lightning, rips infected trees up by the roots, and turns me a coolat shade of blue."

1000

megapocalypse now!

To survive any sort of apocalypse, you can't be a weakling. The creatures and spells from Duel Masters' fifth set have been battle-tested and honed to the ultimate perfection.

Just feast your eyes on these new concepts. The set's survivor creatures share cool abilities, so if one of your survivors has slayer, they all gain the ability. Escaping all that destruction, some creatures have become extra-fast and developed the new speed attacker ability — they can attack the turn they come into the battle zone! A few creatures have the awesome, triple-breaker ability, and the Billion-Degree Dragon is the largest creature yet at 15,000 power!

This expansion set contains 60 cards:

5 super rare ✜
5 very rare ✪
15 rare ★
15 uncommon ✦
20 common ●

Flip through the next five pages for your first look at **Survivors of the Megapocalypse!**

7 — Death Cruzer, the Annihilator
DEMON COMMAND

CREATURE

- When you put this creature into the battle zone, destroy all your other creatures.
- Triple breaker (This creature breaks 3 shields.)

Its only friend is the empty void of death.

13000

---

5 — Gigahail
CHIMERA

CREATURE

- Nature and light slayer (Whenever this creature battles a nature or light creature, destroy the nature or light creature after the battle.)

What it was built out of isn't nearly as disturbing as what was done with the leftovers.

4000

---

5 — Gigaling Q
SURVIVOR / CHIMERA

CREATURE

- Survivor (Each of your Survivors has this creature's ability.)
- Slayer (Whenever this creature battles, destroy the other creature after the battle.)

Did the Megapocalypse create the Survivors, or did it just set them free?

2000

3 — Gigazoul
CHIMERA

CREATURE

- While your opponent has no shields, this creature can't attack.

"Perhaps I went a little too far with the experiment . . ."
—Ballom, Master of Death

3000

---

5 — Horned Mutant
HEDRIAN

CREATURE

- Each nature creature costs 1 more to summon, and each nature spell costs 1 more to cast.

After pulling out its own horns to use as weapons, it can grow a new pair in less than a day.

3000

---

2 — Jewel Spider
BRAIN JACKER

CREATURE

- When this creature is destroyed, you may choose one of your shields and put it into your hand. You can't use the "shield trigger" ability of that shield.

It climbs webs, trees—anything and everything—in search of warm blood.

1000

5 — Scheming Hands
SPELL

- Look at your opponent's hand and choose a card from it. Your opponent discards that card.

"Everyone has secrets. Everyone but you."
—Trox, General of Destruction

---

6 — Sinister General Damudo
DARK LORD

CREATURE

- When this creature is destroyed, destroy all creatures that have power 3000 or less.

"The Fiona Woods will sustain us only for so long. We must push deeper into the Nature realm."

5000

---

4 — Skullsweeper Q
SURVIVOR / BRAIN JACKER

CREATURE

- Survivor (Each of your Survivors has this creature's ability.)
- Whenever this creature attacks, your opponent chooses and discards a card from his hand.

They don't like it when their victims twitch. They're ticklish

1000

1 — Slime Veil
SPELL

- During your opponent's next turn, each of his creatures attacks if able.

"Hey, you're really getting the hang of that. Now make him do a little dance."
—Dark Titan Maginn

---

5 — Vashuna, Sword Dancer
DEMON COMMAND

CREATURE

- While your opponent has no shields, this creature can't attack.
- Double breaker (This creature breaks 2 shields.)

"My specialties are ballet, tap, and merciless obliteration."

7000

---

3 — Wisp Howler, Shadow of Tears
GHOST

CREATURE

- Nature and light slayer (Whenever this creature battles a nature or light creature, destroy the nature or light creature after the battle.)

Although it has no body to feed, it never stops devouring souls.

2000

10 Billion-Degree Dragon
ARMORED DRAGON

- Triple breaker (This creature breaks 3 shields.)

The Megapocalypse will soon begin, deep within the molten core of the planet, the site of the world. It is legendary. And it is...

15000

---

7 Bladerush Skyterror Q
SURVIVOR / ARMORED WYVERN

- Survivor (Each of your Survivors has this creature's ⊕ ability.)
- ⊕ Double breaker (This creature breaks 2 shields.)

Its war cry shreds the clouds. Its blasts shred everything else.

5000

---

2 Blazosaur Q
SURVIVOR / ROCK BEAST

- Survivor (Each of your Survivors has this creature's ⊕ ability.)
- ⊕ Power attacker +3000 (While attacking, this creature gets +3000 power.)

The Blazosaur's roar echoes in the ears of every Survivor.

1000+

---

8 Bolgash Dragon
ARMORED DRAGON

- Power attacker +4000 (While attacking, this creature gets +4000 power.)
- Triple breaker (This creature breaks 3 shields.)

Its suit of armor belches out an electric smog cloud that serves as both camouflage and weapon.

4000+

---

5 Bombat, General of Speed
DRAGONOID

- Speed attacker (This creature doesn't get summoning sickness.)

"Too slow? Do I have tick? or a rocket to go faster?"

3000

---

4 Cannoneer Bargon
ARMORLOID

- ⊕ Shield trigger (When this creature is put into your hand from your shield zone, you may summon it immediately for no cost.)
- This creature can't attack players.

"Why bother aiming? I'll fire in all directions at once."

4000

---

8 Cataclysmic Eruption

- For each nature creature you have in the battle zone, you may choose a card in your opponent's mana zone and put it into his graveyard.

The skies fell, the seas boiled, the cones collapsed. The volcanoes melted, and the forests burned. The planet cracked open, and the Megapocalypse began.

---

3 Cyclone Panic

- ⊕ Shield trigger (When this spell is put into your hand from your shield zone, you may cast it immediately for no cost.)
- Each player counts the cards in his hand, shuffles those cards into his deck, then draws that many cards.

---

3 Kip Chippotto
FIRE BIRD

- When one of your Armored Dragons would be destroyed, you may destroy this creature instead.

Only the Dragons realize that only little birds hold the secrets of immortality.

1000

---

3 Rikabu, the Dismantler
MACHINE EATER

- Speed attacker (This creature doesn't get summoning sickness.)

"I'll leave that ripped open in an instant!"

1000

---

4 Ruthless Skyterror
ARMORED WYVERN

- This creature can attack untapped water creatures.
- This creature can't attack players.

"If you don't kneel before my wrath, you'll certainly kneel after it!"

6000

---

7 Twin-Cannon Skyterror
ARMORED WYVERN

- Speed attacker (This creature doesn't get summoning sickness.)
- Double breaker (This creature breaks 2 shields.)

The first cannon blasts your flank. The second cannon blasts your soul.

7000

5 — Ballus, Dogfight Enforcer Q
SURVIVOR / BERSERKER

CREATURE

• Survivor (Each of your Survivors has this creature's Ⓣ ability.)
• Ⓣ At the end of each of your turns, untap this creature.

To indicate the telepathic link shared by all Survivors, scientists added a code letter to their names.

3000

3 — Calgo, Vizier of Rainclouds
INITIATE

CREATURE

• This creature can't be blocked by creatures that have power 4000 or more.

"Arise, Vizier of Rainclouds. Your lash is the blade of justice."
—Mancha, Radiance Elemental

2000

5 — Gallia Zohl, Iron Guardian Q
SURVIVOR / GUARDIAN

CREATURE

• Survivor (Each of your Survivors has this creature's Ⓣ ability.)
• Ⓣ Blocker (Whenever an opponent's creature attacks, you may tap this creature to stop the attack. Then the 2 creatures battle.)

"My true home is not in the Light realm. It is with the Survivors."

2000

4 — Glory Snow
SPELL

• Shield trigger (When this spell is put into your hand from your shield zone, you may cast it immediately for no cost.)
• If your opponent has more cards in his mana zone than you have in yours, put the top 2 cards of your deck into your mana zone.

4 — Kulus, Soulshine Enforcer
BERSERKER

CREATURE

• When you put this creature into the battle zone, if your opponent has more cards in his mana zone than you have in yours, put the top card of your deck into your mana zone.

Right-side up, it's solar powered. Upside down, it's lunar powered?

3500

7 — La Byle, Seeker of the Winds
MECHA THUNDER

CREATURE

• Blocker (Whenever an opponent's creature attacks, you may tap this creature to stop the attack. Then the 2 creatures battle.)
• Whenever this creature blocks, untap it after it battles.

"Breeze? Nah, Gust? Nah, Tornado? Aw, yeah."

5000

6 — La Guile, Seeker of Skyfire
MECHA THUNDER

CREATURE

• Double breaker (This creature breaks 2 shields.)

Today's weather report: partly cloudy, with an 80 percent chance of being blasted from space.

7500

2 — Le Quist, the Oracle
LIGHT BRINGER

CREATURE

• Whenever this creature attacks, you may choose a darkness or fire creature in the battle zone and tap it. (First choose what this creature is attacking. Then choose a creature to tap.)

"I have developed a devastating new weapon to combat the forces of chaos. I call it 'nap time.'"

1500

3 — Snork La, Shrine Guardian
GUARDIAN

CREATURE

• Blocker (Whenever an opponent's creature attacks, you may tap this creature to stop the attack. Then the 2 creatures battle.)
• This creature can't attack players.
• Whenever your opponent causes a card to be put into your graveyard from your mana zone, you may return that card to your mana zone.

3000

7 — Syforce, Aurora Elemental
ANGEL COMMAND

CREATURE

• Blocker
• When you put this creature into the battle zone, you may return a spell from your mana zone to your hand.
• Double breaker (This creature breaks 2 shields.)

7000

11 — Syrius, Firmament Elemental
ANGEL COMMAND

CREATURE

• Blocker (Whenever an opponent's creature attacks, you may tap this creature to stop the attack. Then the 2 creatures battle.)
• Triple breaker (This creature breaks 3 shields.)

"The Megapocalypse is the first bit of damage I've just begun."

12000

2 — Thunder Net
SPELL

• For each water creature you have in the battle zone, you may choose one of your opponent's creatures in the battle zone and tap it.

"When the device is activated, a net of electricity ensnares our enemies!" —Syrius, Firmament Elemental

Aqua Surfer
LIQUID PEOPLE

6

* ◆ Shield trigger
* When you put this creature into the battle zone, you may choose a creature in the battle zone and return it to its owner's hand.

"Wave goodbye."

2000

Divine Riptide

9

* Each player returns all cards from his mana zone to his hand.

"The Megapocalypse has arrived. It's a bit early, huh?"
—Pokolul

King Mazelan
LEVIATHAN

8

* When you put this creature into the battle zone, you may choose a creature in the battle zone and return it to its owner's hand.
* Double breaker (This creature breaks 2 shields.)

It patrols the Cyber Lords' new undersea city. In exchange, it gets to eat any intruders it finds.

7000

King Tsunami
LEVIATHAN

12

* When you put this creature into the battle zone, return all other creatures from the battle zone to their owners' hands.
* Triple breaker (This creature breaks 3 shields.)

The last time is she's bringing, the receding tidal waves sank three islands.

12000

Lurking Eel
GEL FISH

6

* ◉ Fire and nature creature blocker (Whenever an opponent's fire or nature creature attacks, you may tap this creature to stop the attack. Then the 2 creatures battle.)

The safest place can conceal the greatest danger.

4000

Miracle Quest
SPELL

3

* Whenever any of your creatures finishes attacking this turn, you may draw 2 cards for each shield it broke.

"Search high and low! We must find the Jade Idol! And while you're at it, see if you can find my car keys." —Tropico

Pokolul
CYBER LORD

4

* Whenever your opponent uses the "shield trigger" ability of a shield broken by this creature, you may untap this creature.

The cosmic offspring of Father Time and a motherboard.

2000

Sea Slug
GEL FISH

8

* ◉ Blocker (Whenever an opponent's creature attacks, you may tap this creature to stop the attack. Then the 2 creatures battle.)
* This creature can't be blocked.

The Cyber Lords have high standards of beauty for their creations. They have even higher standards of ugliness.

6000

Solidskin Fish
FISH

3

* When you put this creature into the battle zone, return a card from your mana zone to your hand.

If you look closely enough, you'll notice the rock has eyes. And teeth.

3000

Spikestrike Ichthys Q
SURVIVOR / FISH

6

* Survivor (Each of your Survivors has this creature's ⊕ ability.)
* ⊕ This creature can't be blocked.

"If the Megapocalypse couldn't stop me, what makes you think you can?"

3000

Split-Head Hydroturtle Q
SURVIVOR / GEL FISH

5

* Survivor (Each of your Survivors has this creature's ⊕ ability.)
* ⊕ Whenever this creature attacks, you may draw a card.

"No fair! The more Survivors there are, the stronger they become!" —Miss Titan Gett

2000

Steel-Turret Cluster
CYBER CLUSTER

5

* This creature can't be attacked by fire or nature creatures.

After an onslaught of its armor was performed, a squad of decoy troops was quickly constructed.

3000

CHEN TREG, VIZIER OF BLADES

The next set introduces a fantastic new game mechanic: tapping. Now a creature can forfeit its attack to perform a super-cool skill like Chen Treg's ability to tap any creature in the battle zone.

RAZORPINE TREE

Talk about strength in numbers! For five mana, the Razorpine Tree can start as a hulking 11,000 power if you control all your shields. As your shields get destroyed, the Razorpine Tree grows weaker and weaker.

CRAZE VALKYRIE, THE DRASTIC

An Evolution card that taps two creatures when it enters the battle zone, the Craze Valkyrie can slay one of those neutralized creatures on its attack or slip past big blockers that are no longer active.

SOPIAN

Like a good general, this cyber lord gives orders from the rear and sends others to dive into battle for it. Its tap ability sends a soldier against your opponent's shields that can't be touched.

ENERGY STREAM

Brain Serum costs four mana to draw two cards, and tournament decks include it for card advantage. You can only imagine what those players will think about a cheaper version.

FORT MEGACLUSTER

Want to draw three cards a turn? Five? Ten? This cyber cluster Evolution bestows the card-drawing ability on all your Water dudes, which can give your opponent a handful of problems.

CURSED PINCHER

Not only does this brain-jacker stop an attacker, it destroys it. A blocker with the slayer ability will cause opposing creatures to think thrice about stomping in your direction.

GRIM SOUL, SHADOW OF REVERSAL

Don't throw that dirt into the grave just yet. Grim Soul can tap to return any Darkness creature from the dead pile to your hand. C'mon, you know you're dying to play with it!

PROCLAMATION OF DEATH

Darkness needed more destruction to help out its old standby spells, Death Smoke and Terror Pit. Ask and you shall receive with a shield trigger that destroys an enemy creature of your opponent's choice.

CHOYA, THE UNHEEDING

It might be a pint-sized human, but it doesn't get hurt often. Whenever Choya becomes blocked, the battle cancels and Choya lives to fight another day . . . or, at least, attempts to fight again.

PYROFIGHTER MAGNUS

A 3000-power speed attacker that costs just three mana? What's wrong with that overpowered picture? As a drawback, Magnus has to return to your hand at the end of each turn.

COCCO LUPIA

On its own, it's just a small bird. Combined with a giant dragon, though, Cocco Lupia can help bring your big slugger into the battle zone two turns earlier than your unprepared opponent expected.

MIGHTY BANDIT, ACE OF THIEVES

Remember the days when your 1000-power creature stopped in its tracks at the first scent of an enemy blocker? That's not happening with Mighty Bandit and its ability to throw +5000 onto any attacker.

FAERIE LIFE

Nature has been longing for a good two-mana spell that boosted your overall mana production. Faerie Life is exactly that and more, as it might go off for free as a shield trigger.

INVINCIBLE UNITY

Let's skip the fact that this spell costs 13 mana to play. It gives an unbelievably gigantic +8000 power to all your attackers and beefs them up to triple breaker status! That's game over, for sure.

super rares!

Collecting these rarest of rares wins you only half the battle. See if you can pull off these game tricks for the full experience!

AQUA SNIPER (Base Set)
Little did you know that the Sniper heralds from the land of liquid people, so if you can't find a smaller target, you can trigger one of your evolutions' special effects with it.

LADIA BALE, THE INSPIRATIONAL
(Evo-Crushinators of Doom)
As an evolution, Ladia Bale can attack right away. Surprise and destroy a large enemy creature that's tapped with an even larger 9500-power creature that can block later on.

EARTHSTOMP GIANT
(Rampage of the Super Warriors)
When this giant attacks, you return all the creatures in your mana zone to your hand. You can gain more attackers this way. If you need more mana, play spells to the mana zone.

GALKLIFE DRAGON
(Shadowclash of Blinding Night)
You might not face a Light deck each duel, but when you do, this dragon will become an MVP. Play a single copy and fetch it when you need it with a card like Dimension Gate.

DEATH CRUZER, THE ANNIHILATOR
(Survivors of the Megapocalypse)
Wow, a 13,000-power creature that has triple breaker! Unfortunately, it destroys all your other creatures, so use them purely as mana sources to cast The Annihilator quickly.